TEDDY
Finds A Treasure

Wind-filled sails criss-crossed the bay,
And the sun shone down on a beautiful day.
Teddy and friends relaxed on the sand,
They had swum in the sea and now felt grand.

Bessy and Belle were digging on the beach,
    They had dug down as far as they could reach.
Teddy who was enjoying a quiet little nap,
    Was startled when Bessy cried, ''I've found a map.''

They stretched the parchment out on the sand,
    And looked astonished at a map of the land.
''It's a map of this bay,'' Jimbo said.
    ''X marks the TREASURE,'' Teddy read.

The bears were camped,
 At Whitecliff Bay,
They could see to Portsmouth,
 On a fine sunny day.
They cooked their breakfast,
 On a fire made from wood,
Then donned their life jackets,
 As all sailors should.

"We sail on the morning tide,"
　　　They heard Teddy say,
Then clambered down the path,
　　　To their boat where it lay.
With sails set true,
　　　And bearing compass in hand,
They would find the treasure,
　　　As already they'd planned.

The bears were ready and eager to start,
    And on board they climbed, Jimbo with the chart.
''We'll sail round the rocks then to the cave,''
    Like true seafarers they were all very brave.

Out into the Solent,
        From the Isle of Wight,
The bears in ship-shape fashion,
        Made a wondrous sight.
They passed an ocean liner,
        Going on its way,
And laughed and shouted in delight,
        At the cooling salt sea spray.

Soon they turned the headland,
    And the wind began to drop.
They brought their boat up to the cave,
    And onto the shore did hop.
Forty paces forward,

Thirty to the right,
Then they saw a chest of diamonds,
    That filled them with delight.

Sparkling, glittering diamonds galore,
Teddy reached out with a tentative paw.
On the lid of the chest a faint 'M' they could see,
"It's Captain Morgan's treasure,"
They shouted with glee!

They carried the treasure chest,
    Back to their boat,
Then Jimbo shoved off,
    Once more they were afloat.

They sailed boldly through the rocks,
    And back to the bay,
With a pirate's rich hoard,
    What a wonderful day.

They carried the treasure back to the camp,
  And as daylight was fading they lit a bright lamp.
They put the chest inside the tent,
  Where the lamp so brightly burned,
Then cooked a delicious supper,
  Which they'd well and truly earned.

They sat round the camp fire,
      Drinking honeyed tea,
Talking with great excitement,
      Of their day upon the sea.
Soon they were feeling tired,
      And into their beds did creep.
Tired heads lay down,
      And all were soon asleep.

The birds woke them next morning,
      Singing in the trees,
Turned into a symphony,
      By the humming of the bees.

Teddy's Mummy and Daddy,
      Were coming to take them home,
And on the island ferry,
      They would sail across the foam.

When they arrived back home,
    All the bears of the village were called.

And in respectful silence,
    They listened as if enthralled.
The chest of diamonds was on display,
    For all the bears to see,
But suddenly from the gathering,
    Came a murmur of great glee.

The intrepid bears were bewildered,
　　　And looked about in dismay,
Why were all the other bears laughing
　　　In this curious way?

Then came friendly Policebear,
　　　Who had always been kind to them,
And with a twinkle in his eye,
　　　Explained about the 'M'.

''The 'M' is for marbles,''
    He said with a smile.
The bears roared with laughter,
    They could be heard for a mile.
''Your treasure is very pretty,
    But value, it has none,
So let us make the best of things,
    And have a little fun.''

Teddy laughed, Jimbo guffawed,
    Bessy and Belle rocked and roared.

Grandpa Bear slipped off his chair,
    And Grandma's hat flew in the air.
The bears all laughed and clapped with glee,
    And Bobby Bear fell out of a tree.

A great marbles competition was staged the next day,
And the marbles shared out for everyone to play.

A truly wonderful time,
　　Was had by one and all,
And they finished with a sing-song,
　　In the village hall.